THE ADVENTURES OF MUNFORD

Munford Meets Lewis & Clark

THE ADVENTURES OF MUNFORD

Munford Meets Lewis & Clark

by Jamie Aramini

illustrated by Bob Drost

The Adventures of Munford
Munford Meets Lewis and Clark

Written by Jamie Aramini
Illustrated by Bob Drost
Munford character and concepts created by George Wiggers

Library of Congress Control Number: 2008925624
ISBN: 978-1-931397-55-1

Published in the U.S.A. by Geography Matters, Inc.®
800-426-4650
www.geomatters.com

Printed in the United States of America

DEDICATION

To my parents, Darrell and Barbara Johnson, for always
encouraging me to follow my dreams.

ACKNOWLEDGMENTS

Thanks to Josh and Cindy Wiggers for trusting me with your dream of Munford. I am honored to have the privilege to write this book.

Thanks to Bob Drost for the wonderful illustrations of Munford. He is just as I imagined him!

Thanks to my very patient husband for putting up with me when I'm in writing mode, even though dinner is late and there are no clean socks in the house!

TABLE OF CONTENTS

Chapter 1: Munford Meets a Buffalo

"STOP! STOP!" I yelled loudly. He didn't hear me! I had been sitting there, just keeping to myself . . . and then—BAM! The buffalo ran right out of the river. There I was on top of his head, in for quite a ride!

Had the old bull lost his mind? There was really no way to be sure, and there was really nowhere to go, so I just held on for the ride. He barreled along, two tons of meat at full speed. That was when I saw it.

The buffalo was headed straight for a big camp. Several people were sleeping on the ground. They didn't know what was headed their way.

For a brief second, I took it all in: the smell of wet buffalo, the camp fires reflecting off the tents, the thunder of hooves pounding the earth, the feel of the air rushing by us.

We were getting closer. I closed my eyes as tight as I could. I just couldn't watch. He came to a screeching halt, sliding for a few feet. What had caused the crazy old bull to stop?

A barking dog ran up to us. He looked small next to the bull. Still, all the barking seemed to work! The buffalo slowly backed away. This was my chance! I jumped onto the closest hat. "Go dog!" I cheered. The buffalo turned around. He sulked all the way back to the river.

I saw that there was a man underneath my hat. He called the dog back into camp. "Seaman! Seaman! Come here, boy!" Seaman as they called him, was a big, black Newfoundland with long, shaggy hair. He came panting up to his master. The man leaned down and rubbed Seaman behind the ears. "Good job, Seaman. Good job! You saved our lives, Buddy."

The other men at the camp all cheered for the dog. "That is one brave dog you've got there, Captain Lewis."

Seaman came and laid at the Captain's feet. "Bought him for twenty bucks."

"Not bad since he just saved our lives!"

"Not bad at all," Lewis yawned. "Let's get back to bed, men. We've got an early morning tomorrow." He headed for his tent.

I found what I had been looking for. This was the

camp of Captains Meriwether Lewis and William Clark! I had arrived at last. Captain Lewis took off his hat and settled into his blankets. I stayed on the hat and started to drift off to sleep . . .

Please forgive me! I shouldn't go to sleep yet. I didn't even tell you who I am. My name is Munford. I am a water molecule, two parts hydrogen, and one part oxygen. I am changing all the time.

Some days, I am a big, wet drop of rain. When it gets cold, I become a hard piece of sleet. I really like it when I am a fluffy piece of snow, but the worst is when it gets super cold. Then I turn to ice and get stuck. That is no fun at all!

When things start to heat up, I become a gas. This is called evaporation. Then I can go anywhere the air goes! I'll even catch a ride in a cloud. What a way to travel!

I love adventure. I watched as the first pyramid was built in Egypt. I went to the first Olympic games in Greece, 776 BC. I've sailed with Columbus, painted with DaVinci, and explored with Marco Polo. I keep my eyes open, looking for action!

Action is what led me to Lewis and Clark. I was in the U.S. capital, Washington D.C. Have you been there? It's a lovely city with lots of fun things to do. It was July 4, 1803. I was there to see my Grandpa Gilbert. He had a twinkle in his eye. "I have some news you might want to hear," he said.

"What's that?" I asked.

Grandpa smiled. He knew I was always up for some excitement. "It is top secret. Only a very few know about it."

"About what?" I asked.

"The secret."

"What secret?" I was starting to get upset!

"A group of men are going on an expedition."

Expedition is a word that people use to describe a long trip, usually where a lot of exploring is going to be done.

"What kind of expedition, Grandpa?"

"A big one! The men will travel to the Pacific Ocean, looking for the Northwest Passage."

"What is that?"

"It is a river that is rumored to cross the mountains in the West. If it is found, we can cross the country by boat rather than land. It would save lots of time and money."

I sat for a moment and thought. "So where exactly is the Northwest Passage?"

Grandpa leaned back in his chair and chuckled. "That's the whole point. No one really knows if it is even real. That is why the President has ordered the trip."

This all sounded pretty cool. I wanted to know more. "Who will be leading the men?"

"Captain Meriwether Lewis. His friend William Clark will help him."

I had never heard the names before. "Do you think they will do a good job?"

Grandpa paused for a moment. I could tell he was thinking. "They are just the men for the job. It's going to be a very important trip. Even more now because of the big report today."

President Jefferson had just bought the Louisiana Territory for fifteen million dollars. It started at the

Mississippi River, ended at the Rocky Mountains, and covered over 800,000 square miles.

The United States had doubled in size for only three cents an acre! It was a bargain by today's standards. Still, some thought it was a waste of their hard-earned money.

"So, they will be checking out our new land?"

Grandpa nodded. "At least until they reach the Rockies. They will report about the land's resources. We will know if the President bought good land or bad land. They will make maps of what they see. If they see any natives, they will tell them we now own the land.

"Resources? Maps? Sounds kind of boring."

Grandpa sat up straight in his chair. Uh-oh. "Boring? Boring! These men will be going through strange lands where no American has ever been!

Before 1776

AFTER

"They could run into wild animals, catch a deadly illness, get attacked by natives! What if they get lost? What if they run out of food?

"They will sleep on the ground and in tents with no house to keep them safe! They will leave their friends and families.

"This is about a lot more than resources and maps! These brave men will be risking their lives. Because of their bravery, others will be able to enjoy the new land. It will become a part of our great country."

I was hooked. This was going to be the trip of a lifetime. Of course, that was two years ago, before that buffalo threw me right into the middle of the Lewis and Clark camp.

Chapter 2: Capturing a Prairie Dog

Now, let's get back to camp with the Corps of Discovery. That is the name that was given to the men led by Lewis and Clark. For the first leg of the trip, we went by boat on the Missouri River.

It wasn't easy going. The River was a dirty one. Being water myself, I've seen some doozies. This one topped them all. There were sandbars. There were plants. There were rocks. There were dead trees just floating in the water. The boat was always getting stuck.

Then there was the current. It went along with so

much force; the men could barely paddle fast enough. Sometimes they used long poles and just pushed off the bottom of the river. It was that shallow.

At times, the water was very shallow and filled with debris. The boat just refused to move. The men would get out and tie ropes to the boat. They would pull the boat until it was again in open waters. There were always extra rations for the men after a day like that!

As you can see, travel was very slow. Captain Lewis would often walk along the shore during the day. He gathered plant and soil samples. He sketched drawings of animals and plants, to help us learn more about this new country.

Some of the men came along to get some fresh air. They were also on the lookout for fresh meat. Whatever wild game they could kill would add to what was brought along on the trip. We were walking across an open field when one of the men's feet got stuck in a small hole. Someone helped him out. As the crew went on, more and more feet were getting stuck. The whole field was covered in holes. It was a mess!

Where did all of these holes come from? We didn't wonder long. A strange creature popped its head out of one of the holes. Bigger than a squirrel, it made a sound much like a barking dog. We were all charmed by these odd animals.

After much talk, we decided to capture a "prairie dog" as we called them. It would be sent back to President Jefferson. The men tried to grab them with their bare hands. Those little dogs were a lot faster than they looked. I'm sure I could have caught one. (I am very quick, you know.) Since I am much smaller than the prairie dog,

though, I left it alone. I chose instead to watch as the rest of the men chased the creatures back into their holes.

Almost an hour later, Captain Lewis sent back to the ship for Captain Clark. He wanted him to come and bring some shovels and a few men. "If we can't catch them, we'll dig them up."

When Captain Clark arrived, he and the men with him were smiling and laughing. "You are having some trouble with a squirrel?" They thought it was funny that we couldn't catch one.

We were not amused. "It isn't a squirrel. It's a prairie dog, a whole village of them," Lewis said.

"Squirrel or dog, it doesn't matter. We'll catch it." With that, Clark and his men went to work with their shovels. For a very long time, all they did was dig, dig, dig.

The Corps of Discovery was a mix of young men from all over the growing United States. Most of them were soldiers in the U.S. Army. There were some French men who were hired to help with the boats. Clark's slave, York, also came on the journey. This varied group learned to work together on this day—all because of a prairie dog.

Occasionally, one would stick its head out of one of the holes to see what all the fuss was about. This really made the men mad. "I'll get it!" Someone would shout, and then lunge at the prairie dog. They were just never quick enough to catch it.

Between the digging, the heat, and the fact that we still hadn't caught a prairie dog, the men were getting very impatient.

"This is crazy!"

"We are never going to catch one this way!"

"How long are we going to keep digging?"

"Why are we doing this again?"

"How 'bout we drown 'em?"

There is still some debate among the men about who

made this suggestion. It seems that everyone wants to take credit for the idea. Of course, it was really I who saved the day in the end.

The Captains sent word back to the boat. The rest of the men (except a few to stand guard) came to help, bringing with them everything on board that could hold water. There were buckets, jars, and even kettles from the kitchen.

Several lines were formed stretching from the river to the prairie dog "village." Huge buckets of water were

filled and passed along the lines, then dumped into the holes. There was no whining this time. We were going to catch a prairie dog.

I was thinking about hopping off of Captain Clark (whom I had spent most of the day with). I was going to jump into a water bucket to help out. I really was. My only concern was that I would somehow get stuck in one of those dreadful holes. The thought of that made me feel sick, so I stayed with Captain Clark.

Just as I had made my decision, something awful happened. I lost my grip on Captain Clark's shirt. As he dumped his bucket of water into the hole, I went with it.

"HELP!" I began to scream wildly as I was tossed to and fro. Soon I could no longer see the light at the top of the tunnel. I was dropping further and further down. "HELP ME!"

My life began to flash before my eyes. This was the end. I would spend the rest of my existence at the bottom of a dark hole with a small family of dirty, stinky prairie dogs. I would never see the light of day again.

Just as I thought that my life was over, the tunnel opened up into a small chamber. I landed right on top of a prairie dog. What are the odds of that? The dog took off, scrambling up another tunnel. It was probably going to tell the rest of its friends that they were under attack. I held on for dear life!

What seemed like an hour later, I saw a small shimmer. I could see light. It was a miracle! The prairie dog saved me. It popped its furry little head up out of the ground. The whole group cheered as the prairie dog ran right into a small cage. I let out a sigh of relief. I was alive.

The men kept cheering. Would I be awarded a metal for courage, I wondered? I chased the prairie dog right into a trap. I saved the day . . . a true hero.

Chapter 3: The Teton Sioux

After our run-in with the prairie dog, travel was pretty calm for a while. We paddled against the Missouri River one day at a time. Our goal was to reach the Mandan Indians before winter. We would build a fort and stay until spring.

The further West we traveled, we noticed more and more errors on the map of the country. Captain Clark spent many hours correcting the errors and adding new features. He recorded new rivers, plateaus, and hills. He even named some after people from our group. In the end, even Seaman had a small creek named for him.

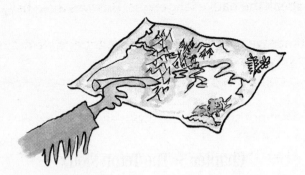

As we traveled on, we met quite a few Indian tribes.
We told them that the United States had just bought the
land that they lived on. We gave them gifts and traded
goods.

Our boat was loaded with gifts for giving. We had
face paint, ribbons, and mirrors. There were thread, fabric,
needles, and thimbles for sewing. There were jewelry and
tobacco. Then there were the beads—over thirty pounds of
teeny tiny beads. I guess the Captains had it in their mind
that the natives loved beads.

So far, things had been going well. The tribes didn't
fight us. We just talked. Some of the men in our group

could speak the native languages. This was a big help.

Sometimes we met a group whose language we did not

know. Then the men would use sign language to talk.

I am not sure that the tribes always knew what we

were saying. They must have, because the Captains seemed

pleased. The leaders of each tribe were given special med-

als. They looked like huge coins with President Jefferson on

them. To accept the medal was to accept our peace.

No one had turned down the medals so far. We were

all nervous about the next stop, though. We were going to

meet with the Teton Sioux. They were the most wealthy and

mighty tribe in the region. The other tribes feared them.

The Captains saved their best gifts for this tribe,

including gunpowder and bottles of whiskey. They hoped

the gifts would keep the Sioux from harming us. They were

known far and wide for bullying all who crossed their path.

I hoped that would not include us.

We arrived early one morning at the home of the

Sioux. There were many of them. They lived in round tents

made from buffalo hide. The tents were called teepees.

Each one was painted with colorful designs.

They welcomed us without a smile. They looked over each gift as they accepted it. They even took a few drinks from the whiskey bottles. Still, they did not smile.

Captain Lewis even fired his air gun. It fired a bullet using compressed air. No powder was needed. Other tribes had been pretty impressed by it. Not these guys.

We were running out of ideas. The Captains were set on making peace with this great tribe. Captain Clark decided to take a few of their leaders on a tour of our keelboat.

It was quite a boat. Sometimes the men called it "the barge," because it was so big. It was 55 feet long and 8 feet wide. Captain Lewis had it built just for this trip. It had twenty oars, each one being 16 feet long. It was a fine boat, to be sure.

The Indians liked seeing it. There were many things to marvel at. They seemed to enjoy their tour. It ended and the Sioux prepared to leave.

The men got back into our canoes to head to shore. There was a sigh of relief from everyone. It seemed that things were going to turn out okay. I was riding in one of the canoes with Captain Lewis and the Sioux leaders.

As we rowed toward shore, I saw that something weird was going on. Our men rowed very slowly, their eyes looking straight ahead. The Sioux men seemed distracted. I looked to the shore. Several of the tribesmen were waiting our return.

One of the chiefs began to speak sharply to Captain Lewis, who had been sitting quietly. I will skip the long pauses taken for translation. The chief said, "Take us back to your boat."

Captain Lewis sat up straight. The canoe rocked. He looked the chief straight in the eye. Our men kept rowing. "I'm sorry. The sun is going down. We must prepare to leave in the morning."

There was a shout from the chief. As we neared the shore, tribal warriors took hold of the canoe. I don't think they were going to let go.

I could see the anger on the face of Captain Lewis. I peeked around one of the men. The men who had been standing around were now lined up in a row. Their arrows were trained on us. I started to sweat.

Back at the boat, the men were ready to attack. They were all at attention, guns ready, facing the canoe. This didn't seem to have much effect on the Sioux. I was trying to decide if I should jump out of the boat.

We were surrounded by arrows at the shore, men in the canoe, and guns from the boat. The guns weren't aiming at us, but I still didn't feel safe.

"You don't want to do this, Chief." Captain Lewis was bluffing. We were outnumbered. Our weapons may have been more powerful. It didn't matter. Fifty men just can't compete with three hundred warriors.

One of the chiefs, Black Buffalo, raised a hand to call the men off. They lowered their arrows, but kept them at the ready. "Perhaps you could stay just a few more days. Our women and children may also see the boat. We do not wish to battle."

Captain Lewis thought for a moment. It could be a trick, but if he said no, there would be a fight. "We will stay."

I let out a sigh of relief. We would make it out alive after all. I was glad Captain Lewis had stayed calm, just like me, calm as can be.

We stayed three more days with the Sioux. We ate and traded and learned about their culture. They asked for more gifts. The captains were more than happy to oblige.

They were especially interested in York, Captain Clark's slave. They had never seen anyone with black skin. They just thought he was all painted up. One chief even tried to wash off the paint. York got a big kick out of this.

By the time we left, the Indians were calling him "Big Medicine." The little ones followed him around wherever he went. They all seemed to think he had magic powers.

York was happy when we left. I think he was worn out from all the attention. I was just glad that we lived. We had survived the Sioux.

Captain Clark named the island next to the Sioux, "Bad Humor." I guess this is how he felt while we were visiting them. He was pleased when we finally left for our next adventure.

Chapter 4: Fort Mandan

The Captains were two very different people. Captain Lewis was reserved and quiet. He stayed busy with his nature journals and samples, leaving Captain Clark to direct the men and plot their course.

Captain Clark was much more outgoing. He liked to tell tales with the men. He wasn't as concerned with the plants and animals as Lewis. Sometimes he did some sketching of them, though.

All the men thought of the two as Co-Captains. I was the only one who knew the truth. Captain Lewis was the only real Captain on the expedition.

Late one night, I overheard them talking about it. It turns out the Army had not agreed to a request by Lewis to make them both captains. They thought that only one man, Lewis, should run the show.

Lewis knew that he needed Captain Clark to balance out his quiet ways. He thought that two leaders would be better than one. I guess he was right, because the trip went smoothly. I don't think anyone found out until many years later.

We arrived at the Mandans' settlement on October 24. We started building our fort right away. There was no time to waste before winter set in.

I hope you remember that your friend Munford (that's me!) is a water molecule. A molecule is two or more atoms joined together. I know it is hard to believe that I am only two hydrogen atoms and one oxygen atom. It is true! (That is where I get the nickname H_2O.)

Like I said before, when it gets really cold, a crazy thing happens to me. I freeze. Somewhere around thirty-two degrees Fahrenheit or zero degrees Celsius, I stop being a liquid. I become a solid instead. In cold weather, I just can't help but become an ice cube.

So, the next time you open your freezer and get out an ice cube, remember that might be me. You might be putting Munford into your water glass. Of course, I might already be in your water glass. You just never know.

I wanted to remind you of all this so you would know what I was doing at Fort Mandan. While the men were building our winter fort, I was frozen. After a hard day out in the cold, stuck to the strings of someone's boot, or frozen to the edge of a coat, I would come in and melt by the fire.

We built many small buildings. A good, sturdy fence was put around it all. Gates were mounted. A lookout post was also built. With nearly fifty men, the fort was completed quickly and just in time. Winter proved to be very cold.

Our first big party at Fort Mandan took place on Christmas Eve. The fort was completely finished, which was cause for a double celebration. Each of the men was given extra rations. Christmas Day was more of the same, with lots of eating and dancing.

The winter of 1804 wasn't all fun. Imagine being cooped up in a small space with fifty people, not just for weeks, but for months. It didn't take long before we all started to go crazy. Of course, it was worse for me, since I was frozen solid.

After hunting and eating, there really wasn't much to do. To ease the boredom, we often went to the Mandan villages to buy, trade, and sell. They were very friendly and went out of their way to care for us. We helped them out in any way we could, too.

Captain Lewis had been trained in medical work before the trip. He studied from Dr. Benjamin Rush, the most famous doctor in the whole country. Dr. Rush taught Lewis how to treat all kinds of illnesses and injuries. He even sent boxes of medicines and equipment to be used on the journey.

All that learning was coming in handy. He was always being called to help out the Mandans. The most common injury was frostbite. He often had to cut off the part of the body that had been affected. This was usually toes or fingers. Yikes!

The Captains met many people with valuable information. Some were natives, some were French, and some were Spanish. Each told what they knew about the land that lay beyond Fort Mandan. Clark used their stories to fill in the blank spots on his map. He even hired a few men to join our party.

One such man was a French fur-trader named Charbonneau. His wife, a Shoshone Indian named Sacagawea, would also come with us. The Shoshone lived further west. The Captains were counting on her to act as translator to her people. They also hoped the sight of her would help them know we were friendly.

One cold February evening, the men had just sat down to dinner. A messenger arrived from the Mandans. Captain Lewis was wanted at the village. One of the women of the tribe was having a baby.

A few of us went along with him, trudging through the cold and snow. We welcomed any chance to get out of the fort. By the time we reached the village, I was frozen

right to the side of the medical supply bag.

The woman in childbirth turned out to be Saca-

gawea. She had been laboring for many hours. The baby

had yet to appear.

I'm not sure how much childbirth training Cap-

tain Lewis had. I'm guessing he didn't plan for that since

our group was all men. He tried a few things, but nothing

seemed to work.

He finally left Sacagawea and stepped out to get some fresh air. I heard him talking with some of the other men. What could they do to help her?

One of the Frenchmen said to try a rattlesnake. His wife, a Mandan, had told him it would help with the labor. "A rattlesnake?" Lewis asked. I could just see him bringing in a snake to bite this poor woman. It didn't sound like the best idea.

"Just crush up the rattles. Does the trick every time."

The Captain didn't reply. He returned to Sacagawea. Still, there was no progress. He dug through the medicine bag, nearly knocking me to the floor. I could tell he was thinking hard.

He went back out and sent one of the men to the fort. They were to return with a rattlesnake tail. (Captain Lewis had several dead snakes in his collection to send back to the President.)

When the man returned, Lewis crushed the snake

tail. He poured the powder into some water. Sacagawea

drank it without a complaint. She's tougher than I. I was aw-

ful glad not to be in that water cup.

You won't believe it. It wasn't ten minutes before I

heard a baby cry. I don't know if it was that snake that did

the trick or not. Maybe the baby was just ready to come

out. All I know is, it sure didn't take long after she drank that

powder.

The little baby was named Jean-Baptiste. He was a cute little boy, that's for sure. As we headed back to the fort, I wondered what would happen to him. Would he be joining us when we left in the spring?

Chapter 5: Grizzly

After the birth of the baby, things calmed down a bit. The men hunted, repaired broken tools, and planned for spring. It was often so cold that no one could leave the fort.

Often we visited the Mandan village. The tribesmen sat around the fire and swapped stories with us. The French told grand stories of their lives back in Europe. Captain Clark talked about the war. The Mandans told us about their rituals, hunts, and travels. My favorite stories from the Mandans were about the grizzly bear.

They explained that the grizzly was a mighty and powerful animal. It had killed many young men who thought they could outsmart the bear. I guess the bear was a little smarter than they expected. They said the grizzly was the biggest, most ferocious animal they had ever seen.

I thought their stories were a little much. A grizzly bear couldn't be that big, could it? Even if it were dangerous, it would be no match for us. We had guns, while the Mandans used only arrows. Little did I know that in just a few short weeks, we would meet a grizzly of our own.

Before we met a grizzly, though, we would stay longer at Fort Mandan. Before the winter was over, our boats were encased in ice. More than one of our men lost a toe to the bitter cold.

It was mid-March when I finally became a liquid again. The river overflowed with melting snow. Green leaves began to sprout on the trees.

After months of testing our patience, spring had finally arrived. The men were anxious to continue our search for the Northwest Passage. It was time to go.

The captains sent some of the men back home. The keelboat went with them, full of goods for the President. Clark included his map of the land we had traveled. Lewis sent his animal and plant specimens, as well as his soil samples. The other men sent letters to their families. There were also gifts from the natives we had met. Our prairie dog, still alive and healthy, was on board as well.

The remaining men left Fort Mandan on April 7, 1805. There were now thirty-four members of the Corps of Discovery, including yours truly. Sacagawea, her husband, and their new baby were also with us. Our plan was to find the Northwest Passage and reach the Pacific Ocean. We hoped to return to Fort Mandan before winter came again.

With the keelboat gone, travel went much more quickly. We rode in smaller boats, which handled the current much better. I rode in a small canoe with Sacagawea.

As before, the men often walked along the shore. This was land that few white men had ever seen. All were eager to explore.

I still remember the first time I saw it. It was large, brown, and furry. It stood by the edge of the river, pawing in the water.

It was a grizzly bear. It was too late by the time the men on shore saw the bear. The grizzly had already seen

them. He had been pawing for fish, but not now. He threw down a fish and charged after one of our men. He showed his huge teeth with an ugly growl. They were in for it.

One of the men shot at the bear with a rifle. It didn't even hurt it. All it did was make that old grizzly mad. He stood up and let out a kind of roar. It was the scariest thing I have ever heard.

I was thanking the heavens that I was watching all this from the safety of the canoe. Someone took another shot at the bear, but it just kept running. The men kept going, too.

I am no animal expert, but I think that running from a wild beast is not a good idea. I guess the men were thinking the same thing. They turned from their course and headed back towards the water.

What were they doing? Surely they wouldn't—oh no! They were leading that grizzly right to the canoes. They must be out of their minds! Now we were all going to die.

I nearly fell out of the boat as they jumped in beside me. One began paddling, as the other pulled out his gun and started shooting. The bear fell down at the shoreline.

He was finally dead. I felt a twinge of sadness for the old bear. Slowly, we paddled up to get a closer look. You wouldn't believe it. The grizzly let out a roar, stood up, and plunged into the water. He was still alive!

I have never seen anyone paddle as fast as those men. One more shot, and the bear finally slowed down. He crawled up onto the riverbank, and breathed his last.

You can bet we waited a lot longer before we went to check things out. There was no way we were getting close. We wanted that bear to be deader than a doornail.

Finally, we got up our courage and paddled over to the bear. He was really gone this time. It took nine shots from expert marksmen and skilled hunters to bring him down. No wonder the Mandans held the grizzly in such high esteem.

Even lying on the ground, he was a scary sight. Of course, Captain Lewis got out his journal. He had to make sketches and measurements. It turns out the bear was nearly ten feet tall. No wonder he was so tough.

We camped nearby that night. Like always, we slept right out under the stars. I kept waiting to hear the roar of a grizzly. I bet I wasn't the only one who didn't sleep soundly.

The Captains slept in a large tent made of buffalo hide. They also shared the tent with Sacagawea, her husband, and baby. I figured a grizzly would tear right through the tent if it wanted. Still, I would have rather been there than outside like the rest of us. You know it would eat us first.

I made it through the night without seeing a grizzly. I was glad to see us pull up camp and move on. Hopefully, that was the end of bear country. Little did I know it was just the beginning.

That grizzly wasn't the last one we ran into. Every time we turned around, it seemed someone was getting chased by another bear. I can't help but think how we had

laughed at the Mandan grizzly stories. I guess they were

right after all.

Chapter 6: Swept Away

There was no time to waste. We were still planning on returning to Fort Mandan by winter. The days became longer and longer as summer drew nearer.

Sometimes the wind became very fierce, causing us to lose control of our boats. A few times, we even stopped our journey long enough to let the wind subside. Our next adventure started on one of those windy days.

The Captains had not yet given us the order to stop. I wasn't on their boat, but I imagine they were probably talking it over. Could we make it despite the wind? Should we go ahead and pull our boats to shore?

I was in another boat with Sacagawea. I grew quite attached to her and her little baby. The Captains had called him "Little Pomp," and the name stuck. He went everywhere tied in a little bundle on his mother's back.

I was sitting on the boat, hoping that the wind would die down soon. Then the unthinkable happened. A strong gust blew across the river, tossing our boat onto its side.

Everything on board was thrown into the rushing Missouri River. Even me! I held on to Sacagawea for dear life. The last thing I wanted to do was to get caught up in the raging river. Then I would be headed downstream, away from Lewis and Clark. Surely I would be lost forever.

I clung to Sacagawea. She was a strong swimmer. "Get back in the boat!" I yelled, but I don't think she heard me.

Why were we still in the water? She was busy grabbing things out of the water. We weren't the only things that had fallen with the boat. The entire contents were now floating in the water. The journals, compasses, and map-making supplies included.

Captain Lewis was shouting frantically from the other boat. I could hardly hear him over the gurgling water. I think he was shouting something about saving his things.

His things! I can't believe he was concerned about *things* while I was about to be lost. I mean, me, Munford, one of the most useful members of the party.

Someone managed to turn the boat upright. As Sacagawea climbed on board, I started to lose my grip. I fell back into the Missouri.

"Save me! Save me!" I shouted.

"Help!" I yelled as loud as I could.

"Captain Lewis! Sacagawea!" They were sorting through the things they had retrieved from the water.

"What about me?" All hope was lost. I looked so much like the billions of other water molecules in the river. How could they even see me? You can't blame the Captains for leaving a man behind. Their only choice was to move on.

The boats became smaller and smaller as I floated downstream. I felt helpless as the Corps of Discovery at last faded from my sight. The current had carried me away.

Currents are one of the down sides of being water. A river current will pull us water molecules along with it. It doesn't matter where we *want* to go. We have to follow the current, not that it is the current's fault. It is really gravity doing all the work. Gravity causes the current to head down stream.

Enough about currents. Let's get back to the story. I stayed with the current long enough to calm down. Once I caught my breath, I grabbed hold of a tree branch along

the shore. I pulled myself up and sat down to rest. How was I ever going to catch up with Lewis and Clark? Despite my small size, my absence would be a great loss to the expedition. Would they go on without me?

The sun was warm on my back as I rested on the tree limb. I slowly drifted off to sleep. Dreams filled my head of Captain Lewis, grizzly bears, Little Pomp, the Northwest Passage.

We just came upon the Pacific Ocean when I woke up. I wasn't at the Pacific, or still on my tree branch. I was floating through the air. The hot sun had caused me to evaporate. Evaporation is the process where water is heated from a liquid state into a vaporous state.

Usually, when I've been evaporated, I travel by air. One of the great things about air travel is that you don't have to travel in groups. It's just you rolling along across the wide, open spaces.

The major problem is that you have to go wherever the wind takes you. There are wind currents just like there are river currents. You can't exactly tell a strong wind that is blowing towards Canada to turn around and head south. It just doesn't happen. Trust me, I've tried.

Maybe that is why some water molecules prefer traveling by way of a good river. They say the river is more reliable than the wind. At least you know where it is going. Perhaps.

I would much rather travel alone on the wind than be in a river any day. All that pushing and shoving and fighting to be on top just gets to me. You saw what happened when I fell in the Missouri.

Oh, and nothing is worse than the rapids. The pushing turns into a real brawl. That is when things get really scary. I'm all for adventure, but I never said anything about pointless fighting.

So there I was, floating on the breeze. This was by far the best way to search for Lewis and Clark. I could see the entire countryside stretched before me. Rolling hills stretched before me, with the Missouri River snaking its way through them.

There, in the distance, further up the river, I spotted Lewis and Clark. They were just pulling their boats to shore. The time to set up camp was getting close.

I had to get close to that camp. I tried to think up a plan as the sun started to set. The temperature began to drop. Night was coming.

I couldn't stay a vapor forever. Cooler temperatures cause me to change my form. *Condensation* is the word scientists like to use. I went from a vapor to a liquid. Joined up with other water molecules, I was now part of a cloud.

A cloud is always nice and roomy at first. As we traveled along, we picked up more passengers. Molecule after molecule joined us. Things started to get crowded. A toe was stepped on. There was an elbow to a rib cage. Voices were raised.

This was life in a cloud. It didn't last long, though. Once a cloud gets so full, it can't hold another drop of water. Everyone was elbow-to-elbow, and starting to get a little bit grumpy. The sky was dark now. Our little cloud hid the moon's face from view.

Someone else tried to join us. There just wasn't any
more room. RRRRRRRIIIPPP! The cloud split wide open. I was
headed for the earth, and fast.

Chapter 7: The Water Cycle

KERPLUNK! I landed on a rock. I was part of a rain-drop, along with other water molecules. We were all holding on to each other for dear life as we fell to the ground.

What a ride! I said goodbye to the rest of the rain-drops. There was no time to chat. I was still on a mission to catch up with the expedition.

Being water really opens up a lot of different ways to travel. A wild dog licked me off of that rock. Then I couldn't go anywhere. I was just stuck in his stomach, waiting to be, well . . . digested. I worried that he might carry me far

off course. He ended up carrying me for a few miles while I

weaved my way through his belly.

The dog had to use the bathroom. The next thing I

know, I'm being expelled onto a tree. Boy, was I ever glad to

get out of there. I could go my whole life without ever see-

ing the inside of a dog again.

It wasn't long before a bird came along. I grabbed onto its feather, hoping to catch a view of the camp. No such luck. He brushed me off onto a flower petal before I had a chance to see anything.

The sun was high in the sky now. I started to warm up. I turned from my liquid state back into a vapor. I floated off through the sky.

It was night before I spotted the Corps of Discovery. I could see their camp by the light of the moon. How was I going to get there?

I knew that as the night temperatures dropped, I would change. Would I join up with another cloud? Would something else happen?

As it turns out, I didn't join a cloud. When I started to cool, I condensed right on the side of one of the boats. If you had seen me, you might have called me "Dew." Personally, I don't like being called "Dew." After all, my name is Munford.

Now I was a liquid and no longer a vapor. I was on the boat and ready to go. I was thankful I was away from the group for only a few days. Hopefully I hadn't missed too much action.

I can't tell you how happy I was to be back with the group. The further we traveled, the closer we became. I no longer felt like just another member of the expedition. I felt like part of a family.

I wasn't the only one that felt that way. When we came to a fork in the river, the Captains decided which path to travel. We all thought they were choosing the wrong path. Even so, we took the fork chosen by the Captains. Our respect for them both kept us from complaining or rebelling. They said that was the way to go, so we followed. No questions asked.

At Fort Mandan, we had been told about a huge waterfall further up river. If we had indeed taken the right path, we would eventually find it. Weeks went by and still no waterfall. Although it was never spoken, many began to wonder. Had the Captains chosen correctly? Had the river fork we chose been the Missouri? Or had we traveled miles down the wrong stream? Should we have blindly trusted two men who had never been this far west?

On June 13th, our questions were answered. At first we heard the gentle buzzing of water over rocks. Soon the gentle buzz turned into a loud rushing noise. By mid-morning, the rushing had turned into the loud roar of falling water.

As we turned a bend in the river, we saw what all the fuss was about. We reached what the Indians called the Great Falls. *Great* was something of an understatement. It was by far the largest waterfall that I had ever seen. Clark

thought that it was around eighty feet high and three hundred yards wide.

I got dizzy just looking at the Great Falls. I've never really enjoyed waterfalls that much. Just the thought of it seems pretty wild. Poor little water molecules were peacefully floating along the river. Can you see it? Then, suddenly, they slip over the edge, plummeting to the bottom. Then they are thrown into a rushing torrent of water and dashed against hard, sharp rocks.

It makes me sick. Some of the other H2Os really get into that kind of thing. They say you haven't really lived until you've done it. "What an adventure!" they say. I've lived plenty, thanks. I'm always up for a good adventure, but a waterfall? That's just plain crazy.

It wasn't just me who was overwhelmed by seeing the Great Falls. It was bad news for our whole group. Our boats would never safely make it across the water. We would have to make a portage. A *portage* is a common thing on trips like ours. All of our boats, equipment, and supplies must come out of the water. We then carry them around whatever is in our way, in this case the Great Falls.

We knew that this would happen. From what the Mandans said, we figured we would be about half a day on our portage. We made carts from trees and loaded up as much as we could. The rest was buried so we could get it on the way back.

Horses would have helped. There were none,

though, so the men were forced to drag everything. I did

what I could to help, but being so small, I couldn't carry

much. Instead, I hitched a ride on one of the carts.

The ground was covered with sharp rocks. There were thorns, sticks, and brush. The moccasins that the men wore did little to protect their feet. By the end of the first day, their feet were blistered, bleeding, and bruised, and we still had quite a ways to go. This was going to take a lot longer than half a day.

The June weather made the portage even harder. It was hot. I mean really, really hot. Every time I turned around, it seems like I was on the verge of evaporating. I finally found a cool spot under the brim of a hat, where I could safely rest without the heat getting to me.

The heat was hard on the men, too. They took frequent breaks to cool off. They also drank a lot of water. The Captains gave extra rations every night to keep up the morale.

As if the heat weren't enough, there was also another problem—the mosquitoes. These weren't your everyday kind, either. They were huge! They were everywhere. Sometimes they were so thick we could hardly see to go forward. All of the men were eaten up with bites. I was glad that I was small enough to escape the notice of these pesky bugs.

This was life during our portage around the Great Falls. We were dragging hundreds of pounds of supplies over rocky terrain in scorching heat, fighting mutant mosquitoes. It was the hardest part of our journey so far.

Chapter 8: Flash Flood

We were two weeks into the portage, and things still weren't looking up. One thing the Mandans failed to warn us about was the storms. It was like nothing we had ever seen. One moment we were trudging along, the sun's rays beating on our backs, not a cloud in the sky. Then, in what seemed like an instant, black, billowing thunderclouds rolled into sight. Lightning lit up the sky. Thunder roared around us.

The thunderstorms around the Great Falls came with little warning. When they did come, it was with a vengeance. Often large pieces of hail were mixed in with the rain.

It was during one such storm that we nearly lost part of our party. Captain Clark decided to walk directly along the river. I joined him, as well as Charbonneau, Sacagawea, and their baby.

It was a pleasant day. Clark was gathering some soil and rock samples for Captain Lewis. He also carried his gun, in hopes of getting some wild game. We were all enjoying the walk, admiring the beauty of the waterfalls beside us.

This section of the river flowed with a steep ridge on both sides. The ridge blocked out much of our view of the sky. Because of this, we didn't see the storm until the last minute.

At the first sound of thunder, I jumped into Captain Clark's shirt pocket. I knew what was coming and didn't want to get washed away by the rain. It poured out of the clouds like it was dumped from buckets. Huge pieces of hail pounded into the ground.

The waterfall gushed at twice its normal volume. The river began to rise out of its banks. Captain Clark shouted to the others. "We must get up the ridge!"

Charbonneau went first, pulling Sacagawea with him. A lightning bolt struck beside them, startling everyone. Our climbing became more frantic.

Captain Clark brought up the rear of the party. He pushed Sacagawea forward, balancing his gun in one hand. Everyone was quickly drenched from head to toe.

A huge gust of wind blew. Sacagawea slipped, and stumbled to the ground. She began to scream. I peeked out of the Captain's pocket, just in time to see Little Pomp's carrying pack go bouncing into the river.

"I've got him!" shouted Clark over the roaring river and raging rainfall. Sure enough, there in his arm was the baby. His clothes went with the pack, but he was still here. He cried at the top of his lungs, but it looked like he was mostly unharmed.

Charbonneau helped Sacagawea to her feet. "We must keep moving. The river still rises!" She took her baby in her arms and held him close. We continued up the ridge.

"Over here!" Captain Clark pointed to a rock overhang protruding from the earth. We scrambled in that direction as quickly as we could. I tried to stay calm as I bounced around inside the pocket.

We finally made it under the rock. Everyone stayed close together for warmth as the storm continued outside. The river rushed by below us, taking everything in its path with it.

Sacagawea soothed Little Pomp, who was still crying from it all. "Thank you, Captain, for saving the little one's life," Charbonneau said. "If you hadn't acted so quickly, he would have been washed away with the river."

"I'm just sorry I couldn't get his pack as well. We will have to build one and find some new clothes when we get back to camp." He patted the baby on the head. "At least you are okay, Little Pomp."

Charbonneau smiled. "I am afraid, though, sir, that you have lost your hat."

The Captain reached up and touched his head. "My hat! My favorite hat! What will I do without it?" We all had a good chuckle over the Captain's missing hat.

"I won't be able to replace that hat until we return to Saint Louis. I should just be happy that I will be alive to return there."

When the storm subsided, we headed back to camp. York met us half way. "Captain. You are alive! We thought you had been killed in the flash flood."

"Don't worry. I'm alive, too. Me, Munford." I spoke up from my post in Clark's pocket.

York ignored me. "We have been searching for you, but the storm made it impossible to see for more than a few feet."

The Captain laughed. "A few feet? It felt like we couldn't see a few inches. We are none the worse for the wear. Only Little Pomp has lost his britches, and I'm afraid I've lost my favorite hat."

York replied, "But no lives were lost, sir?"

"No. Our party is all in good health. We must get back to camp and find some dry clothes and a warm fire to dry us out."

The men cheered as we walked into camp. They were happy to see us alive and well. We were glad to be back.

From then on, the Captains were careful to watch for signs of impending weather. We stayed far from the riverbank if even the smallest fluff of a cloud was in the sky. Sacagawea sewed up new clothes for Little Pomp, but no one ever found Clark's hat. Luckily, he was able to borrow a hat from one of the other men.

After our brush with death, the portage returned to normal. It was still miserable. It was two more weeks before we reached open river again. We could now put our boats on the river and travel on.

Instead of getting right in the river, the Captains chose to take a break. It had taken a little over a month of hard labor to make the portage. The men were exhausted.

Much of our equipment was damaged from the rough terrain or the deadly hailstorms.

We took several days to recoup. We repaired supplies. We sewed up new moccasins. We rested our aching muscles.

We even celebrated Independence Day on the fourth of July. The men shot some extra meat for the occasion. It was a great celebration. It helped to keep our minds off of what might be ahead of us. We tried not to think of the long journey we might be facing. We were just thankful to have the portage over with.

Chapter 9: The Continental Divide

The extended portage put us behind schedule. The men were growing more and more anxious everyday. We wondered if we would return safely to Fort Mandan before winter.

We were still following the path of the Missouri River. The water level had started to drop. In fact, it was so shallow in places that our boats sometimes had to be pulled along from the shore. It was no longer the wide river we were used to, but had narrowed quite a bit.

We would soon reach the Northwest Passage. The Missouri would flow into another river. This new river would flow into the Pacific Ocean. If the two rivers were not connected, we hoped that only a short portage would be needed.

Every member of our crew was not so optimistic. Some believed that there was no Northwest Passage. They believed that the Missouri was just a dead end. Still others believed that we were lost entirely, perhaps not even on the Missouri.

It wasn't long before our boats could no longer travel the Missouri. It had simply become too narrow and too shallow. The river divided up into several smaller streams, one of which we knew would lead to the Pacific.

Captain Lewis decided that a scouting party should be formed. This party, led by the Captain himself, would travel ahead of the main group. We would see which path was the best and shortest for the rest to follow.

I decided to head out with the scouts. I figured if any adventure was going to happen, we would be the first to see it. I didn't want to miss a thing.

It was August 12, 1805. We left camp before sun up. The cool of the morning quickly slipped away as the August sunlight began to streak the sky. The heat didn't slow the men down. They hiked along the main stream. I rode along under the brim of the Captain's hat.

The stream kept getting smaller. The further we went, the less it resembled the mighty Missouri. It was starting to look more like a little creek.

Wait. Where did it go? The creek ended just ahead of us. It seemed to vanish in a pile of rocks. "Here we are, men!" The Captain shouted as he ran ahead of us.

He pulled back some brush from the rock pile.

Sure enough, water was bubbling up out of the rocks and

flowing downstream. This spring was the beginning of

the Missouri River. We had followed it all the way to the

source. Captain Lewis called it "the headwaters." This tiny

little spring came up out of the ground and became the

narrow creek we had followed. The narrow creek trickled

into the wider stream. The stream flowed along, picking up

more water from other creeks and streams, until it became

so wide that it formed the Missouri River. All of this started

right here where we were standing.

The men gave a little cheer. The Missouri River had

been full of danger and excitement. More than once, we

nearly lost everything. More than once, lives were almost lost in the powerful current of this great river. Yet, here we were, standing at the end. We had conquered the Missouri River. The men took turns drinking from the fresh spring water.

If there were a Northwest Passage, we were in it. From the stories we heard, another river should start very close by. After giving it all a moment to soak in, we pressed on.

Full of excitement, we crossed over the small ridge that lies before us. Everyone was talking. Could this be it? Had we found the Northwest Passage? We must be getting close to the ocean.

We reached the top of the ridge. Silence came over us. We were in awe. From the ridge top, we could see for miles. There were many huge mountains. Compared to these, the mountains back home were more like foothills.

These were massive, dark mounds of earth and rock. They were so tall that the tops, covered in snow, touched the clouds.

The mountains, towering above us, were almost scary. Someone might as well have put up a big warning sign: "DANGER! DO NOT CROSS!" As for the Northwest Passage, all hopes were dashed. I hated to be the one to have to tell the President this bit of news.

Captain Lewis let out a sigh. We all wondered what he was thinking. Would we attempt to cross the great mountains? Would we continue in search of the Pacific? Was he disappointed? I think he was mostly amazed. No matter how terrifying they might be, those mountains, standing there all proud, strong, and immovable . . . were something to see.

Captain Lewis explained to us where we were. It was the Continental Divide. Every continent has a divide, and this was the Continental Divide of North America. A divide separates the directions that the rivers flow. On the other side of the ridge, all rivers flowed west instead of east. From this point on, any water would be pushing us along instead of pulling us back.

The Continental Divide was also the western border of the Louisiana Territory. It was the end of the land purchased by President Jefferson. No American had ever been this far. The mountains we saw were called the Rocky Mountains. I thought the name was fitting.

We returned to camp in silence. We all had a lot on our minds. I shivered at the thought of crossing those snow-capped mountains. I'm sure the other men were thinking the same thing. The good Captain Lewis, though, was not afraid. He walked with his shoulders back and his chin up. I could tell the wheels in his head were turning.

Back at camp, everyone wanted to know what had happened. In the privacy of the tent, Lewis talked things over with Captain Clark. Captain Clark then emerged to address the entire group. "I'm sorry to say men that there is no Northwest Passage." The men let out a gasp.

Clark kept talking. "From the maps I have seen and the information I have gathered, this is the most likely place for it to be. Instead, the scouts discovered today that no large river flows at the base of the Missouri. Instead, a mountain range stands in its place. We will not let this slow us down. We must still find the Pacific.

"We believe that the great ocean lies just over the mountains. It will be hard work to cross the mountains, and we will need to find packhorses. I believe if we can find the Shoshone Indians, they will have horses to sell us. Sacagawea is a Shoshone, and she will help us find her people and obtain what we need.

"The men who were with Lewis today may tell you that the Rockies look like they cannot be crossed. They will tell you that the tops were capped in snow and rose up into the clouds.

"I do not deny these claims. But, men, we have made it this far. We have traveled a river that many say could not be traveled. We have stayed together safely against all odds. Let this new trial set before us be no different. We *will* cross the mountains. We *will* find the Pacific. Sleep soundly, because in the morning, we will prepare for our journey."

Chapter 10: The Shoshones

The Captain was right when he said we were going to need horses. We would need too much food and too many supplies to try crossing the mountains without them. At Fort Mandan, we were told that the Shoshones were famous for horse-trading. They were the only ones that could help us. The only problem now was how to find them.

Things were different in the West back then. You couldn't just open up the phone book and find out how to get a hold of somebody. We couldn't even ask around to see where the Shoshones might be. To make matters worse, we knew that native tribes were always on the move. It was possible that we could see their camp one day, only to find them gone when we finally reached it.

Our only hope was Sacagawea. She was a Shoshone who was captured by another tribe and traded to the Mandans. She was only a young girl when she left her people, but we hoped she could remember something that would help us find them.

Some things looked familiar to her. A rock here, a hill there. It still wasn't enough. The Captains tried to be patient, but there wasn't much time. We had to find horses and get started over the mountains. If it got any colder, we would have to wait until spring.

The Captains divided up the group into smaller sections. Each went a different way, looking for any sign of human activity. We would report back to camp at sunset.

I went with Captain Lewis. This time, I was perched on top of his hat. I could see for quite a ways up there. I kept my eyes peeled. Those Shoshones had to be somewhere.

We went over the ridge we had visited the day before. There was a low valley at the base of the mountains. Captain Lewis thought he might have seen an Indian trail in the valley. We headed that way.

We found the trail pretty quickly. Worn from years of use, it wound through a grove of trees. It looked well traveled. The men walked quietly, trying to listen for unusual sounds.

It was mid-morning when Captain held up his hand. He signaled for us to be still. In the distance, we heard women talking. I could not understand their native language, but I listened as hard as I could.

We slowly crept closer to the talking. I was the first to see them through the tree leaves. It was three Indian women gathering food. They were digging up roots from the dark soil.

We were in luck. Here were just the people we had been looking for. The women would lead us to their tribe.

Captain Lewis led us out into the open. The women looked at us with alarm. One of the women dropped her basket and made a run for it. The other two, an older woman and a young girl, did not move. It was like they were frozen to the spot. They were frozen with fear, I guess.

The last thing Lewis wanted to do was scare anybody. He laid his gun down to show them that he was friendly. I thought this was awfully brave, myself. If I were big enough to carry a gun, you bet I'd hang on to it.

The Captain was probably wishing that he had brought Sacagawea along. If these women were Shoshone, she could just tell them what we wanted. Instead, Lewis and one of the men did their best to talk with them using sign language.

They just stared blankly. I don't think they were getting it. Then Captain Lewis reached into his bag and pulled out some beads. He gave the women beads and mirrors and other little gifts. They smiled and eagerly took what they were given. I think any person can understand that a present means peace.

The Captain explained as best he could that he wanted to meet with the tribe. He needed horses. He would be willing to pay, of course. The women smiled, and happily led us in the direction of their village.

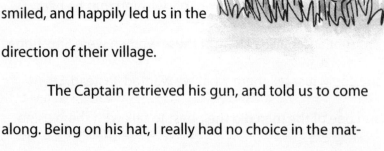

The Captain retrieved his gun, and told us to come along. Being on his hat, I really had no choice in the matter. If I were one of the men, though, I wouldn't have gone.

These women could have been leading us to our death.

Perhaps they didn't understand what the Captains had said.

Maybe it was all just a trick.

Maybe I was being silly. I don't know. I did a quick

head count. There were only nine men in our group. There

was no telling how many men might be waiting for us back

at the village. Shouldn't we at least go back first for rein-

forcements? What about Sacagawea? Shouldn't we try to

find her? At least she could talk for us.

Captain Lewis must have been a little more trusting.

Really, I think he only had one thing on his brain: horses. He

wasn't even thinking about our lives.

We kept walking. We followed the same trail that we

had been on. We must have walked for at least two miles.

Still there was no sign of anyone else. Did they even know

where their village was?

Wait. What was that? I caught a glance of something out of the corner of my eye. Was it a deer, perhaps, or maybe a squirrel?

I blinked. When I opened my eyes back up, sixty natives on horseback surrounded us. They weren't just any natives, either. These guys looked like warriors to me.

No one moved. I held my breath, trying not to attract attention. The men sat calmly on their horses as they aimed their arrows right at us. There was no doubt now. These were warriors for sure.

I tried not to panic, but I was having trouble breathing. I sensed a slight tremor in the Captain's hand as he placed his gun on the ground. He held his hands up in the air. The other men followed suit. I kept thinking about those reinforcements. I knew we should have gone back for them.

No matter how scared we all were, I had a feeling Lewis was still just thinking about one thing: horses. The warriors themselves were skinny, almost sickly looking.

Their horses, on the other hand, were healthy and well behaved. Lewis eyed them. I had to wonder if horses were worth all of this.

One of the Indians came riding up to the front. He was dressed much fancier than the others. "The chief," Lewis whispered.

The chief started talking very rapidly. He said things that I didn't understand. He must have sensed our confusion, because he turned to the oldest woman. He said something to her.

She said something, which made the chief frown. Then she handed him her basket. On top of the roots she had gathered were the beads she had received from us. The chief thought for a moment. He then waved to his warriors, who lowered their arrows. It looked like we might make it after all.

Chapter 11: Horses!

We followed the Chief to the Shoshone village. It was a small village, with very few teepees. The women and children looked thin, much like the warriors. Grazing beside the village, though, were many horses.

We were taken to the hut of the chief whom we had met earlier. His name was Cameahwait. One of our men, Drouillard, communicated with him through a kind of sign language.

It had been many hours since breakfast. All the chief had to offer us was a meal of boiled root and dry berries.

Another tribe had recently attacked the Shoshones. This tribe had guns—much like the ones we carried—to kill and to steal supplies. Now the people barely had enough food to survive, and not enough places for all of their people to live.

I guess that is why they didn't want to trust us. Can you blame them? We carried guns that looked just like those that were used to attack them. Perhaps we were even friends with the enemy tribe.

Still, Cameahwait offered what little food he had. He wanted to make peace with us. Captain Lewis and the other men were the first white people they had ever seen. The women and children stared much like the Mandans had done at York.

Drouillard explained that there were more white men coming. We came first to find horses for the group. We meant no harm. We just wanted to do business. We could help the tribe by trading valuable goods for horses.

I couldn't tell if the chief really believed us or not. I think it was hard for him to trust a man with a gun. Finally, after two days, he agreed to take us back to the rest of our party. If we had told the truth about them, he would then make us a deal on horses.

We started the several mile walk back to camp early in the morning. I was glad that we would be back with Captain Clark and the other men. We missed their company. I also remembered that there was safety in numbers.

We arrived at the meeting place that afternoon. Our tents and some of our supplies were set up. There were even a few campfires still smoldering with heat.

The only thing was . . . no one was there. Not a soul. It looked like the camp had been abandoned. Worse yet, it looked like we had lied.

Cameahwait, for the second time since we had met him, began talking very fast. The other Indians spread out, searching the area. I panicked. If they believed we had lied to them, they would kill us all right here. Why did I come with Lewis in the first place? I should have just stayed with everyone else where it was safe.

One of the warriors returned. He had seen no one.

This was the end, I thought. We had made it so far, and for nothing . . . Wait a minute. What is wrong with me? I am Munford, grandson of the great adventurer Gilbert. I am brave. I am strong.

"Men, give your rifles to the Shoshones." Captain

Lewis spoke with authority.

Had Lewis gone crazy? Our only form of defense,

and he wanted us to give it away. The men, nearly as fright-

ened as I, laid their weapons on the ground.

Lewis explained that we would all put on Shoshone

capes. If it were a trap as Cameahwait expected, we would

be mistaken for Indians and killed as well. This seemed to

ease the chief's mind. I, for one, was glad that there was no cape small enough for me. What if a rogue tribe did attack the Shoshone? Our men would be killed as well.

What happened to Captain Clark, after all? Maybe he and his men were attacked. Perhaps that is why they were not at our meeting place.

We camped overnight waiting for Clark and the rest of the expedition. No one slept very well. The Shoshones still thought that it could be a trap. The rest of us were wondering what would happen if Clark never showed up.

We sat around the campfire early that morning, waiting nervously. We dined once again on dried berries and boiled roots. From the looks on their faces, I think the men found this meal to be lacking in flavor. Cameahwait

talked with other members of the tribe in quiet tones. I

think he was trying to decide what to do with us.

We heard them before we saw them. Seaman came

running through the woods with a bark. Boy, was I happy to

see that dog. Captain Clark came out first, with Sacagawea

not far behind. As soon as she saw us, she began shouting

and dancing wildly. Well, I missed her, too, but you didn't

see me dancing any jigs.

The Shoshone were her people, the same ones she

was kidnapped from many years ago. She was home. She

gave hugs to some of the men as tears streamed down her

face.

We were relieved! Sacagawea's joy put everyone at ease. The men took off native disguises and returned the capes to their owners. The Corps of Discovery had just made it through another run-in with danger.

We all returned to the Shoshone village. It was time to get down to business. We needed horses. The Captains and some others went into Chief Cameahwait's hut.

It is always hard to bargain with someone who doesn't know what you are saying. The translation process in this case didn't help much. The chief would speak. Sacagawea would translate it into French. Her husband would then translate it from French into English. It took a few minutes to get the message across.

We were in the middle of all this translating when something strange happened. Sacagawea jumped up and shouted. She ran to Cameahwait and threw the blanket she was sitting on around his shoulders. She hugged him as tears streamed down her cheek.

What was going on? Hugging the chief of the tribe isn't exactly normal behavior. I personally thought that the woman had lost her mind. The long trip with a small baby had done her in.

She finally calmed down and started talking to her husband. She had to repeat herself several times. Finally, Charbonneau understood. "He is her brother!" He said.

Chief Cameahwait was Sacagawea's brother. Hard to believe, I know. She was taken as a young girl from her tribe by another tribe. She had traveled all over the West. What were the odds that she would ever find her people again

and that her brother would be chief? She was overjoyed.

Things went better than expected. Of course Cam-

eahwait was anxious to help the men who had brought his

sister home. He was also happy to receive the things they

had in trade for the horses. Captain Lewis was able to trade

twenty dollars worth of clothes and knives for three horses.

Some of the other men in our group also traded for horses.

The Shoshones were fortunate to get these needed sup-

plies, and we were grateful to have horses to help us over

the mountains.

Chapter 12: The Mountain

The rest of our time with the Shoshones was spent preparing for our journey forward. We talked to the elders of the tribe about the best route to cross the mountains. We sent a few scouts out to get familiar with the territory. We knew that what faced us would not be easy.

Our only option was to travel by land. The few waterways were too narrow for our boats. We wanted to find the easiest, safest route to follow.

One of the tribe elders told us of a trail through the Bitterroot Mountains, a branch of the Rockies. It was very rough, with little food along the way. Still, tribes who came from the coast to hunt buffalo often used it.

The same elder knew more about the mountains than anyone else. We called him Old Toby. The Captains employed him to be our guide across the mountains. We needed all the help that we could get.

We spent the next few days readying our supplies. We smoked meat and fish. We made new luggage out of animal hides to use with the packhorses. We traded with the Shoshones for more horses.

On the day that we left, there was a sense of sadness around the camp. Sacagawea had decided to continue forward with us rather than stay with her people. The women of the tribe gave her new jewelry and beads. Everyone kissed the baby goodbye.

No one knew how dangerous this trip might become. The truth was, we might not ever make it through the mountains. We were all wondering the same thing. Would we live through the Bitterroot Mountains?

We began our travels with the sunrise. We had twenty-nine new horses loaded down with food and supplies. It was early September and the weather was perfect. Ahead of us, though, the mountains were already capped with snow.

Do you remember Fort Mandan? How I was always frozen? It was freezing in the mountains, too. Most of the time, I was frozen solid to poor Old Toby's coat.

This isn't exactly my favorite way to travel, but what could I do? The only way I could melt would be to get inside Toby's coat. His body heat would warm me right up. Sounds like a good idea, right? It would have worked. The only problem was how to get unstuck from his coat. Oh well, some things in life we just have to accept.

The Shoshones told us it would only take five days in the mountains. Boy, were they wrong. It took us a little longer than five days. Try eleven. Perhaps eleven doesn't sound like much to you, sitting in your cozy, warm house with a full belly. To us, though, it seemed like a hundred days. Since I was frozen solid then the men must have been near freezing themselves. Bbbrrrrrrrr! It makes me cold just thinking about it.

The path through the mountains was very narrow. We were forced to travel in a single-file line for most of the time. The horses carried most of the supplies, but the men had to lead them up the hills. The horses weren't always co-operative. I don't blame them. Sometimes the men had to get out front and pull the horses up the hill. This was very tough work. I didn't think it could get any worse.

I was wrong. Things could get worse. We were three days in when the first snowflakes began to fall. At first, the snow falling made for a pretty sight. Next thing you know, we were in the middle of a blizzard.

We were forced to come to a complete stop because no one could see through the blinding snow. Of course, you can't really blame the snow. It wasn't like my fellow water molecules wanted to make the trip harder. It just kind of happened that way.

To make matters worse, Lewis and Clark had brought only enough food to last five days to cross the mountain and two in case of an emergency. That leaves four days without food.

Four doesn't really sound like much, does it? Stop and think about it for a second. How long was it since you had your last meal? It was probably not more than a few hours ago. Four days is MUCH longer than a few hours!

It was pretty bad for the men in the expedition because they were cold and tired, too. A curious thing happens when you are walking up a mountain nearly frozen solid. You become hungry—much hungrier than you would normally be.

There were no plants to eat. There were no animals to hunt. The animals probably had more sense than to go up the mountain in this kind of weather.

Finally, the Captains decided to kill a horse to eat. The men didn't like horsemeat, but it tasted good right then because they were so hungry. By the time we got out of the mountains, we had eaten three horses to keep from starving.

The men were starting to lose their morale. The first signs of spring didn't seem to give them much hope. Their

aching stomachs kept them down and out. The Captains did their best to keep their spirits up.

Not to brag, but I think I had the best attitude out of everyone. Maybe it's because I wasn't hungry. One of the great parts of being a water molecule—no food needed. While the other men whined and complained, I stayed cheerful.

We slowly made our way down the mountain. The weather started to warm up. The snow on the ground turned into a kind of wet mud. Soon it disappeared com-pletely. The warmer weather meant that we were getting closer to living things, which meant animals. Animals meant food. We were all ready and waiting for a good meal.

Things got even better for me as we went down the mountain. I started to melt. I was no longer stuck to Toby's coat. I was back on the move. What a relief! I could once again be a help to the group. Up until now, you see, I had felt a little useless. There is nothing worse than not being able to help out in times of trouble. Now I was ready to face adventure.

Captain Clark took a small group of men ahead of the rest of the party. They were to look for signs of life and food. The Captains were hoping that they would run into a friendly native tribe. Hopefully, this tribe would be able to supply us with food. They might even be able to point us towards the Pacific Ocean.

I stayed behind with Captain Lewis and the others. Remember the last few times I went out with a scouting party? It seemed like the scouts were always getting into trouble. Nope, this time I decided to hold back. Don't get me wrong. Usually I'm the first to volunteer for a dangerous scouting assignment. After being frozen for over a week, I really needed a break.

Chapter 13: The Nez Perce

It was a day or two before Clark returned. I was with

Lewis, who rode at the front of the party. We were all anx-

ious to hear whatever news Clark brought.

"Lewis! Today is the day!" Clark came riding towards

us on his horse. There was an almost happy tone in his

voice. This was not something we heard much of lately.

"Have you found the Great Ocean?" Lewis asked.

Clark came up alongside Lewis. "It isn't that day,

Captain." He lowered his voice to a whisper. I sure was glad

I was close enough to hear what they were saying. "We

did find a large Indian tribe, just upriver. They should have enough food to feed us all."

"Are you sure? I don't want to tell the men unless we know for sure. We cannot get their hopes up. They are near starving as it is. If this doesn't work out for some reason, telling them would be cruel."

Clark nodded. "That's good advice, my friend. We shall not tell the men. They will know when they get there."

I was excited now. The men would be glad to see people again, not to mention food other than horse. I just hoped that all would go as planned.

The sun had crossed the sky by the time we reached the Indians. When the men saw the little huts lining the Clearwater River, they began cheering loudly. Everyone knew that those little huts meant food.

There were several Indian women gathered outside the huts, working and keeping an eye out for the children. At the sound of our men cheering, they all dropped what they were doing and looked up.

What a sight to see. Our men were skinny and covered in dirt. Our clothes had been mostly new before our trek into the mountains. Now they were barely hanging on. Some of the men had lost fingers to frostbite. The horses looked just as bad, except they were about to collapse from the weight of their loads.

We met with the chief of the tribe. The only way to communicate was through sign language. We were the first white men they had ever seen. Our guide, Toby, had told us that these people were called the Tribe of the Pierced Noses. Their name in French was Nez Perce.

We were in a kind of sticky situation. Our men were hungry, tired, and weak. The Nez Perce could kill us and steal our things. We wouldn't be able to put up much of a fight.

We were loaded down with what most tribes only dreamed of—guns and powder. With those things in their possession, the Nez Perce would become the most power-ful tribe for many miles. Needless to say, we were at risk.

I guess the Captains knew this. They were extra nice to the Nez Perce. They traded more than the usual trinkets and beads. They gave whatever it took to get food for the men.

The Nez Perce didn't try to hurt us. Really, I don't think they were much better off than we were. Even though they didn't have much, they were still willing to trade.

The Nez Perce lived on the Columbia River, world-famous for its supply of salmon. The people pretty much lived on salmon. Anyway you can think of salmon, they ate it. They ate raw salmon, roasted salmon, fried salmon.

Mostly, though, the salmon they ate had been dried so it would last longer.

Boy, were the men glad to eat that salmon. They ate that fish as fast as they could. They ate and ate and ate. They ate until I don't think their bellies could hold one more bite.

Can you guess what happened next? That's right. The men hadn't been eating much lately. Then they ate all that salmon, and ate it in a hurry. It wasn't long before the men got sick.

We stayed with the Nez Perce for a while. We couldn't pack up our things because the men were all too sick. They had to keep running to the bushes. Heaven only knows what they were doing in there. I have a feeling it wasn't pretty.

There were only two people in the whole lot of us who didn't get sick. Sacagawea was one. I think she was a

little more careful about how much and how fast she ate.
The other one was me. That's right, me, Munford. I didn't
get sick once. Of course, I am so small I'd be more likely to
be eaten by a salmon than to eat one myself.

There is a lesson to be learned in all of this. The lesson is not to eat too much salmon. It was a hard thing to
learn, but it wasn't soon forgotten.

We spent several more months on the Columbia.
Do you know what? No one from the Corps of Discovery
ate any more salmon. Those fish would be jumping right
up out of the water. It was like they were begging us to fish

for them. It didn't matter. No one wanted a thing to do with that salmon. The men would go hungry before they had any more of that fish.

After a few days, things started to look up. The men were spending less and less time in the bushes. It was time to move on. The Captains still wanted to get to the Pacific Ocean as soon as we could.

The Nez Perce had been so generous with their food. The men were truly thankful. But everyone was ready to get out of there, away from that salmon. The fastest way to travel now would be on the Columbia.

The only problem was that we would need boats. It was a good thing that we were surrounded by big trees. The captains ordered all the men who were well enough to start making canoes from those trees.

The next morning, the men rose early from the village and traveled to a nearby grove of trees. It was time to carve some canoes. I was up first, ready to get started at the hard day's work. You can call me a lot of things, but you can't call me lazy. (Well, I guess you could *call* me lazy, but it just wouldn't be true.)

All the men were moving a little slowly. They were still sore and tired from crossing the mountains. They were still a little on the sickly side from all that salmon. I did my best to help out, but there is only so much I can do by myself.

A few hours into the morning some of the Nez Perce came out to watch us work. They laughed as we slowly carved at the huge tree trunks. This kind of upset me. We were doing the best that we could under the circumstances. I just don't like people who make fun but don't help out. I was about to give them a piece of my mind when one of them began shouting at the others.

They started a fire right there in one of our tree trunks. Oh, the nerve of some people. I watched in horror

as the wood began to burn. What were they thinking? It

had taken us a good hour to cut that tree down. If we had

planned on burning it, we could have just left it up there.

The other men looked just about as dumbfounded

as I did. Everyone watched it burn for a few minutes. Then

the Indians slowly poured water over what used to be our

tree trunk, now roasted to a crisp.

As the fire went out, an amazing thing happened.

The tree actually looked like a boat. The same canoe would

have taken us many hours to carve out. They did it in less than half the time.

We all felt a little silly that we hadn't thought of it before. We were supposed to be the "civilized" group. We were supposed to be smarter than these people, who were called "savages." I guess the only lesson we learned from the Nez Perce wasn't about salmon. They also taught us to never assume that we knew better than someone else. It was an important lesson for me, as well as the rest of the Corps of Discovery.

Chapter 14: The Pacific

The next day, we departed on our newly burned boats in hopes of soon reaching our final destination—the Pacific Ocean. This was our first travel by boat since crossing the Continental Divide. The Columbia River pushed us ahead instead of pulling us back. This made travel faster than it had been on the Missouri.

Fur traders had once visited the territory we were now in. Of course, they had all reached it by boat from the ocean. No one from the east coast had ever been there by traveling across the land.

We were now able to see landmarks that others had marked on our maps. This was a great change. Instead of filling in blanks, we could now see where we were going by the map.

We knew that we were getting closer and closer and closer to the Pacific Ocean. Sure, we were worn out from the thousands of miles already traveled. We were so close to our goal now that we could literally taste it. The river water was flavored with the slightest hint of salt. The Ocean was close for sure.

The land was much different than what we were used to. We were no longer surrounded by flat plains, but by an overcrowded forest. Huge trees filled with wildlife grew tall along the banks of the river. We often came across brilliant waterfalls. The whole area was damp, covered by what seemed like constant light rain, a kind of mist.

There were many more birds in this part of the country, too. There were birds in the water, such as ducks, geese, and swan. I liked to see the birds. The men, on the other hand, were soon annoyed by the loud noises they often made.

The thing I remember most about this stretch of our trip was the rain. I know that I said it before, but I'll say it again. It seems like the rain never stopped. Lewis and Clark and the rest of the men didn't enjoy the rain. Sacagawea and I were the only ones who really appreciated it. It seemed she was always thankful for whatever happened on the trip. I guess because, for her, it was like coming back home.

I would like to say that I was just naturally thankful and cheerful, too. That wouldn't be entirely true. In reality, I liked the rain because I got to meet all kinds of other water molecules. Back on the Great Plains, it was very dry. There hadn't been a lot of molecules to meet. Now there was

water everywhere.

I remember one morning as being really special. We

were traveling down the Columbia. It was, as usual, raining.

I was resting on the shoulder of one of the front oarsmen

in the lead canoe. I liked being towards the front so that I could see what was going on.

Anyway, I was just sitting there, resting. I would have been rowing, you know, but I am so small I didn't think I could hold the oar. Otherwise, I would have been right in there working hard. I decided it would be better for me to just blend in. I kept an eye out for any hostile natives or wild beasts.

So I was just sitting there when this pretty lady, a water molecule like myself, came to rest just a few inches from me. She smiled. I thought I better say something or risk seeming rude. "Hello there! My name is Munford. What brings you to this part of the country?"

She laughed. "A rain cloud." She spoke with a bit of an accent.

You can imagine that I felt a little silly. A big rain cloud had filled the sky and a raindrop fell beside me. So

I asked the water molecule where it came from? It should have been pretty obvious. "A rain cloud? Huh . . . never would have guessed it. What's your name?"

"Lily. I am from England. Of course, I've traveled all over. What are you doing with this big group of humans?"

I was quickly trying to recall exactly where England was located. Wasn't that somewhere in the Eastern Hemisphere? England is a part of Europe, actually. I think.

I wanted to make a good impression on this pretty lady from another part of the world. I told her all about the Corps of Discovery. "I am on a very important expedition with the great adventurers, captains Meriwether Lewis and William Clark. The mighty government of the United States of America has commissioned us. We are to explore the heretofore unknown terrain of the mysterious Western United States, so recently purchased by the great President Thomas Jefferson. Together, we form the Corps of Discovery. Having traveled this immense country in search of the previously undiscovered Northwest Passage, which we now know does not exist, we are currently continuing on to the Pacific Ocean.

Lily looked at me with a blank stare. Maybe I had said too much? "Did you say something about the Pacific Ocean?"

Had she heard me at all? "Yes."

"Okay, I wasn't quite sure what you said. The Pacific Ocean is just a bit ahead. I was there only a little while ago. You should be there very soon."

Wow! The maps were right. We were getting close. "That is great. I mean, that is excellent news, ma'am. I will be sure to report it to one of the captains. They will be very pleased, I'm sure."

Lily smiled. "Yes, well, it was very nice to meet you, Monsfur."

"Munford." I can't believe she couldn't remember my name.

She blushed. "Oh . . . well, sorry."

"It's okay. Not a problem. Nice to meet you, too."

Lily smiled. "I think I'll drop off into the river now. It will make for a more comfortable trip. Maybe I'll see you again sometime."

With that, she was gone. I didn't even get a chance to say goodbye. Of course, on an important trip like this, you can't let a little setback like that get you down. You just

have to look ahead and not worry about the past. It was hard, though. I really think that she liked me, don't you?

I didn't think about Lily for long, though. She was right. The Pacific Ocean came into view.

Captain Clark was the first to see it. "Ocean in view!" He shouted. We all strained our eyes to see it.

Sure enough, there it was. Through the mist, we could see the vast ocean stretching out before us. The waves crashed onto the shore before rolling back out with the current.

It was a beautiful sight. All of the men, as well as Sacagawea, let out a cheer. Even Little Pomp seemed to understand. He clapped his little baby hands with glee.

We had reached the Pacific.

Epilogue: Going Home

It was November 18, 1805. Over one year after the Corps of Discovery had left St. Louis, we reached our final goal. We had conquered the great continent of North America.

As I watched the cold, blue waves crash against the rocky shore, a sense of relief washed over me. I had made it. Under Lewis and Clark, I had embarked on one of the greatest adventures of my lifetime. Just a little ol' water molecule. There were so many times when I didn't think I would make it—the prairie dog, the near-fight with the Lakotas, our frozen trek over the mountains—but I did.

I knew that it was time for me to move on. The Corps of Discovery still had to make the trip back to their homes, but other adventures were waiting for me elsewhere. I found myself not wanting to leave the Corps of Discovery. These men, Sacagawea, the baby . . . we had been through so much together. We had become a family.

As I dropped off into the Pacific Ocean, I waved goodbye one last time. It was only a moment before the Corps of Discovery was out of sight.

This certainly isn't the last adventure I will ever go on. I hope you will catch up with me the next time I'm out in the wild. Don't ever forget Munford—The World's Most Daring Water Molecule. Where will I end up next?

A Note from Grandpa Gilbert

Munford's adventure with Lewis and Clark was of great importance to the history of the United States of America. Most importantly, the Corps of Discovery staked the claim of the United States on the Oregon region. This opened up the area to American settlers who would later come to live there by way of the Oregon Trail.

In addition, the writings, sketches, and maps made by Lewis and Clark provided invaluable information on the geography, plants, and animals of North America. The expedition recorded about 300 new plants and animals that were unknown to science at that time. They gathered important information on the ways of life of about 50 different native tribes of the land.

The teamwork, courage, and overwhelming strength displayed by the Corps of Discovery is a great example of the spirit of the people of the early United States. The story of Lewis and Clark is more important to history than the things these men accomplished. Their contribution of a truly great adventure, full of true danger and overcoming obstacles, will most likely outlast the maps and scientific information these men gathered.

Lewis and Clark Expedition Facts

Objectives:
- Finding the Northwest Passage (possible water route across North America to the Pacific Ocean)
- Establish American claims to the territory
- Study flora, fauna, native cultures, and geography

Accomplishments:
- Created detailed river maps
- Charted the weather
- Discovered 178 new plants
- Discovered 122 new animals
- Established diplomatic relationships with native tribes
- Mapped true course of the Missouri River
- Gained extensive knowledge of the geography of the West
- Influenced establishment of fur trade

Corps of Discovery:
- Comprised of 33 soldiers and 9 civilians
- Deaths: 1 (illness - probably ruptured appendix)
- Dates: May 14, 1804-September 23, 1806
- Total miles traveled: over 8000
- Average miles traveled per day:
    up the Missouri River: 15
    north to Mandan village: 7-10
    back from Mandan village: 30
- Greatest distance traveled in a day: 50 miles (downstream)
- Total cost: $38,722

Author's Note

Sharing the Vision of Munford

I met Josh and Cindy Wiggers, the fine folks behind Geography Matters, while I was still in high school. Their kids and I went to church together and were becoming fast friends. It wasn't long before I went to the Wiggers house for a visit. Josh made quite an impression on me. First, he insisted that everyone call him Uncle Josh. Second, every conversation, it seemed, ended up turning into a geography drill. "What is the smallest country in the world? What is the capital of Zambia? What country is located between France and Spain?" Needless to say, all of these questions were a little overwhelming, but I kept going back for more visits and more geography drills.

Uncle Josh began telling me about a vision he had of a character he named Munford. He had first dreamed up the little water molecule many years before in a moment of inspiration while driving on the highway in the rain. Because Munford was water, he could be anywhere at anytime in history. By following his adventures, kids could learn about science, history, and geography. There would be almost no limit to what Munford could do. The only problem was that Uncle Josh hadn't been able to find a writer that was a good match for Munford. He had heard that writing was a hobby of mine, and wanted me to give it a try. I'm not sure exactly why he chose to take a chance on me. I was only a sophomore in high school! He must have liked my sample chapter, though, because he asked me to finish the book and then write another (about the Klondike Gold Rush).

It has been nearly seven years since I first set pen to page and wrote Munford's first adventure. In that time, Uncle Josh and the rest of the Wiggers family have became like a part of my extended family. Geography Matters has grown and flourished as one of the best homeschooling publishers on the market today. Munford himself has gone through many changes, thanks to multiple revisions and improvements.

Munford, who is actually a water molecule, is often referred to and portrayed as a water drop. A water drop is actually made of many water molecules, so I took some artistic license by calling him a drop. It is easier to understand and visualize Munford as a drop rather than a teeny, tiny, molecule that cannot be seen with the naked eye.

He is now ready to meet the world! My hope for Munford is that he will teach your children without them even realizing how much they are learning. That way, if they ever have the chance to meet Uncle Josh, or someone like him, they will be able to answer those pesky geography, history, or science questions with pride.

About the Author

Jamie Aramini is the author of *Eat Your Way Around the World*, an international cookbook for kids, and *Geography Through Art* with Sharon Jeffus. Jamie graduated co-valedictorian of her high school class and was a Kentucky Governor's Scholar. Now she is a stay-at-home wife and mother whose interests include organic gardening, cooking, and making stuffed animals from old socks. Jamie can't wait to start homeschooling her one-year-old son, but in the mean time entertains herself by teaching a writing class to the very creative students at the local homeschool co-op. Visit Jamie's website at www.jamiearamini.com

About the Illustrator

Bob Drost is an illustrator, cartoonist, drawing instructor, and author of the 3-D drawing guide *Everything Starts with a Smile*. His work has appeared on TV commercials, in books, newspapers, and magazines. Known as Mr. D, his hands-on drawing presentations in classrooms, school assemblies, and libraries consist of 3-D art lessons in a simple, successful, and fun format. To contact Mr. D email him at bobdrost3d@gmail.com.

Other titles published by Geography Matters

The Adventures of Munford: The Klondike Gold Rush by Jamie Aramini

Geography Through Art by Sharon Jeffus and Jamie Aramini

Eat Your Way Around the World by Jamie Aramini

Eat Your Way Through the U.S.A. by Loree´ Pettit

Cantering the Country by Loree´ Pettit and Dari Mullins

Galloping the Globe by Loree´ Pettit and Dari Mullins

Trail Guide to U.S. Geography by Cindy Wiggers

Trail Guide to World Geography by Cindy Wiggers

Trail Guide to Bible Geography by Cindy Wiggers and Diana Wiebe

Uncle Josh's Outline Map Book or CD-ROM by George Wiggers and Hannah Wiggers

Laminated USA and World Color Wall Maps

Laminated Outline Maps

Mark-It Timeline of History

Historical Timeline Figures CD-ROM

Bible Timeline Figures CD-ROM

Contact us for our current catalog,
or log on to our website.
Wholesale accounts and affiliates welcome.

(800) 426-4650   www.geomatters.com